Bluebell Woods

Honey's Midnight Show

For Mum with love X
L.N.

For Hannah and Emma
with love XX
R.H.

STRIPES PUBLISHING LIMITED
An imprint of the Little Tiger Group
1 Coda Studios, 189 Munster Road,
London SW6 6AW

Imported into the EEA by Penguin Random House Ireland,
Morrison Chambers, 32 Nassau Street, Dublin D02 YH68

A paperback original

First published in Great Britain in 2012

Text copyright © Liss Norton, 2012
Illustrations copyright © Rebecca Harry, 2012

ISBN: 978-1-84715-229-9

The Forest Stewardship Council® (FSC®) is a global, not-for-profit
organization dedicated to the promotion of responsible forest management
worldwide. FSC® defines standards based on agreed principles for responsible
forest stewardship that are supported by environmental, social, and economic
stakeholders. To learn more, visit www.fsc.org

10 9 8 7 6 5 4 3 2

Bluebell Woods

Honey's Midnight Show

Liss Norton

Illustrated by Rebecca Harry

LITTLE TIGER

LONDON

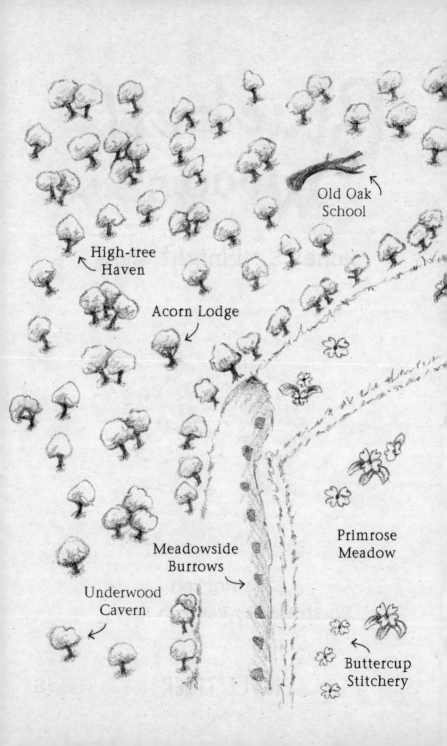

Old Oak
School

High-tree
Haven

Acorn Lodge

Meadowside
Burrows

Primrose
Meadow

Underwood
Cavern

Buttercup
Stitchery

Chapter One

"Come on!" called Honey Pennyroyal.
"We'll never get to the boat at this rate!"

She and her friends Natalie Hollyhock,
a hedgehog, Evie Morningdew, a squirrel,
and Florence Candytuft, a rabbit, were on
their way to sail their boat. Honey waited
for them to catch up, then they skipped
across Primrose Meadow paw in paw.

"It's a perfect afternoon for sailing,"
Natalie said happily. A light breeze was
rippling the grass in the meadow and
stirring the leaves of the trees.

Bluebell Woods

They reached the Stepping Stones
and jumped across, then hurried along the
bank of the Babbling Brook to the willow
tree where they moored their boat.

"What are you all wearing to the
Summer Ball?" asked Florence.

"I've got—" Honey began. She broke
off suddenly and looked around. "What's
that noise?"

Florence pricked up her long ears.
"It sounds like bells," she said. "But
where's it coming from?"

A clump of white-flowered yarrow up
ahead began to shake, then two dormice, a
boy and a girl, popped out from underneath
it. The girl, who looked about the same age
as them, wore a multicoloured dress dotted
with tiny silver bells that jingled as she
walked. The boy seemed a little older.

He was wearing a gold, glittery jacket, red trousers and a black top hat.

"Hello," Honey called.

The dormice hurried towards them, smiling. "Hello, we've heard there's a village around here," said the girl. "Do you know it?"

"Our village is just across the Babbling Brook," said Honey, exchanging glances with her friends. "Shall we show you the way? My name's Honey," she added, "and these are my friends, Evie, Florence and Natalie."

The girl twirled round, setting her bells tinkling. "I'm Mirabelle Eyebright."

"And I," said the boy, taking off his hat and making a low bow, "am Cosmo Eyebright. We belong to Eyebrights' Extravaganza, a troupe of travelling players."

"Oh!" Honey cried, clapping her paws. "Actors!"

"Please can you tell us about Eyebrights' Extravaganza," said Evie, as they led the way to the village.

"Well, there are ten of us," Mirabelle said, "and our mum and dad are in charge. We travel from village to village putting on shows."

"Will you be doing one here?" squeaked Honey excitedly.

"Yes," said Cosmo. "It takes place on

Friday at midnight. We've come on ahead of the rest of the troupe to put up posters." He threw open his coat and the friends saw that it was lined with pockets, some long, some wide and all of them bulging with hidden treasures. Cosmo whisked a poster out of a deep pocket and unrolled it. "See? 'Eyebrights' Extravaganza proudly presents *Lost in the Night*.'"

The friends gathered round to read the colourful poster.

"It sounds amazing," Honey said.

"It's a new show," Mirabelle explained. "Friday night will be our first performance!"

They reached the Stepping Stones and crossed over into Primrose Meadow.

"What a pretty place!" exclaimed Mirabelle. "So many flowers!" The primroses that gave Primrose Meadow its name had finished flowering for the year, but it was full of yellow buttercups now.

Cosmo produced more posters from his pockets. "Where shall we put them?" he asked, fishing out a ball of string. "We'll tie them on so they don't blow away."

"One can go on that hazel bush," Evie suggested, pointing. "Nearly everyone passes it on the way to school."

"And you can put one on the hedge near my nest," said Honey.

The friends scurried to and fro across Primrose Meadow, helping the Eyebrights hang their posters.

"All done," said Cosmo, as they hooked the last one over a low branch near the

Stepping Stones, before crossing the brook. "Let's go and meet the caravans."

As they hurried through Bluebell Woods, the friends looked out for the travelling players' caravans. Suddenly, Honey spotted a patch of bright blue between some nettle stalks. "Over there!" she cried.

"It's Mum and Dad!" exclaimed Mirabelle, running towards two dormice pulling a blue caravan with red wheels and a curved roof stacked high with baskets. "Eyebrights' Extravaganza" was painted in gold letters on its sides.

"Hey, Mum and Dad, we've found the village," called Cosmo.

"And we've made some friends already," added Mirabelle. She introduced Honey, Natalie, Florence and Evie.

"Delighted to meet you," Mr Eyebright boomed. "I'm Eduardo Eyebright, the founder of our troupe." He was a very round dormouse, almost as wide as he was high, and he wore green trousers, a waistcoat and a hat with a red feather.

Mrs Eyebright, who had golden fur, wore a crimson dress that brushed the ground as she walked. "Hello, girls," she said, smiling broadly.

"Let me introduce the World Famous

Fantastic Flier, Tatiana!" cried Mr
Eyebright, gesturing towards the caravan.

At first Honey couldn't see who he
was talking about, then she spotted a very
young dormouse fast asleep between two
baskets on the caravan's front seat.

"Tatiana's our sister," Mirabelle said
proudly.

The friends exchanged puzzled glances.
Tatiana looked about the same age as
Florence's little sister, Rosie, and it was
hard to see how anyone so young could be
world famous.

"Why is the show on at midnight, Mr
Eyebright?" Florence asked.

"Because, my dear," he replied,
lowering his voice mysteriously, "there's
magic in starlight, twinkling lamps and
shimmering costumes."

Honey smiled to herself as she imagined the lights and colourful costumes shining under the starlit midnight sky.

Two more caravans, one green, one red, trundled into view. They were being pulled by a plump rabbit and a large mole.

"The rabbit's Caspar Corncockle," said Mirabelle. "And the mole is Josiah Beechbark." Hearing their names, the two animals gave cheery waves.

Lastly, two yellow carts appeared, piled

high with baskets. They were pulled by
another rabbit and mole, while a dormouse
pushed one cart from behind.

"Leonie Corncockle and Veronica
Beechbark," Cosmo said. "And the
dormouse is Mum's cousin, Freya
Hawthorn."

"Show us the way to the village,
Mirabelle," said Mrs Eyebright.

"Come, troupe!" cried Mr Eyebright.
"Our campsite awaits!"

Chapter Two

The caravans and carts set off again towards the Babbling Brook.

"How will we all get across the stream?" Mirabelle asked.

"By ferry," said Honey.

"And we can help you push the caravans and carts there," said Florence.

Honey and Mirabelle scampered round behind the Eyebrights' caravan and threw all their weight against it. Evie and Natalie helped push the green caravan, Cosmo pushed the red one and Florence helped with both carts, running from one to the other when their wheels got stuck in ruts.

"Gosh, your caravan's heavy, Mirabelle," Honey panted, pushing with all her might.

"At least the ground's dry," said Mirabelle. "When it's been raining, the caravans get stuck in the mud and it's really hard to shift them."

Soon, to Honey's relief, they reached the Babbling Brook. Mr Willowherb's raft was moored on the other side, and he was sitting on the bank in the sunshine.

"Hello," he called. "Who have we got here, then?"

"Travelling players!" Honey called back. "Can you take them across, please, Mr Willowherb? They're putting on a show in the village on Friday."

Bluebell Woods

Springing on to the raft, Mr
Willowherb punted across the stream.
"I hope Luke and Lily will be better by
then," he said, as he secured the mooring
rope. Luke and Lily Willowherb were in
the friends' class at school.

"Are they ill?" asked Natalie, concerned.

"They've just caught a summer cold,"
said Mr Willowherb.

The friends helped to push the
Eyebrights' caravan on to the raft.

"There's room for one of the carts,
too," said Cosmo. They guided it aboard,
then squeezed in around it.

It didn't take long to reach the opposite bank. They unloaded the raft quickly so that Mr Willowherb could go back for the rest of the troupe, then watched as the raft crossed the brook again.

It took three journeys to get everyone across but, at last, as the sun began to set, all the travelling players reached Primrose Meadow. Mrs Eyebright paid Mr Willowherb with free tickets for the show.

"Lovely!" he exclaimed. "Thank you."

"Follow me!" cried Mr Eyebright, pointing ahead with a flourish.

The caravans and carts bounced across the meadow.

"Where will you camp, Mirabelle?" Honey puffed, hoping she wouldn't have to push the heavy caravan too much further.

"Dad will find us a good spot," replied Mirabelle.

They hadn't gone far before Mr Eyebright called, "Halt!" The caravans and carts lurched to a stop beside Foxglove Hollow.

"The perfect place," announced Mr Eyebright. "We will set up the stage in the bottom of this dip, and the audience can sit on the slopes to watch."

"You're near my nest!" Honey squeaked excitedly. "We'll be neighbours."

"Is there a village school?" asked Mrs Eyebright. "I'd like Mirabelle and Cosmo to go to lessons while we're here."

"Yes," replied Honey. "Shall I call for them tomorrow morning?"

"I'd like that," Mirabelle said, smiling.

"Tatiana's awake," said Cosmo, lifting

her down from the caravan seat.

"Hello, Tatiana," chorused the friends.

The little
dormouse rubbed her
eyes sleepily. "Will
you come to watch
our show?" she asked.

"Yes," said Evie. "We can't wait!"

"Would you like to see inside our
caravan?" asked Mirabelle.

"You bet!" the friends exclaimed.

Mirabelle and Florence took the
baskets off the caravan seat, then Mirabelle
folded down the back of the seat. She lifted
a set of wooden steps out of the caravan
and placed them on the ground. "Follow
me!"

They climbed the steps and squeezed
through the narrow doorway.

"It's tiny," Evie said, gazing round.
"Even smaller than Ralph's barge." Ralph
Reedmace was a water vole they'd met in the
spring when they were out on the river.

Along the caravan's back wall was
a padded bench, with cupboards below.
Pots and saucepans hung from the curved
ceiling, and the floor was covered by a
patterned rug.

"Where do you all sleep?" asked
Natalie, puzzled.

Kneeling on the bench, Mirabelle undid a hook. A bed flapped down from the wall. "Cosmo's bed," she said. She made a second bed drop down beneath the first. "This one's mine and Tatiana sleeps here." She patted the bench. "Though we sit on it during the day."

Mirabelle flipped a catch in the opposite wall and another bed flopped down, a double this time. "This is Mum and Dad's bed," she said. "And watch this." She turned it over and it was transformed into a table.

"What a lovely home!" Honey exclaimed.

"It is," agreed Mirabelle.

"Whoa, it's almost dark!" cried Evie, looking out of the window. "It's time we were going."

Bluebell Woods

"See you tomorrow, Mirabelle," the friends said, as they scrambled down the caravan steps.

"Fancy them camping near my nest!" Honey said, as they headed for home. "I'll be able to watch them rehearsing from my bedroom window."

"You'll be able to see what they're having for dinner, too," teased Evie.

Honey laughed. "It's great having them here, though, isn't it?"

Natalie nodded. "I think Mirabelle will be a good friend."

"Yes," agreed Evie. "And Cosmo. I'd always thought actors would be a bit big-headed, but they're not like that at all."

"I can't wait to get home and tell everyone about the show," said Florence.

"Me neither!" the others cried together.

Bluebell Woods

"Guess what!" Honey whooped, as she raced into the living room. Her mum and dad were sitting on the sofa, drinking tea, and her older sister, Hattie, was reading. Harvey and Albie, her twin brothers, were sniggering together in a corner.

"What, darling?" asked Mrs Pennyroyal. "How was your sailing trip?"

"We didn't go because we met some travelling players. They're putting on a show in Bluebell Woods."

"Brilliant!" Hattie exclaimed. "When is it?"

"Friday," said Honey. "It's a play called Lost in the Night." She pulled a flyer out of her pocket. "Look!"

"Is there any fighting in it?" asked Harvey, flicking Albie's ear.

"We're not going if there's no fighting," Albie said, pulling Harvey's whiskers. "We don't want to watch soppy singing and dancing."

"We will all go to the show," said Mr Pennyroyal. "And that includes you two."

"Yippee!" cried Honey.

"Boo-ee!" Harvey and Albie groaned.

"Tell us all about it, Honey," Hattie said, taking the flyer. "I'm looking forward to it, even if Harvey and Albie aren't."

Chapter Three

Honey got up extra early next morning and helped herself to a hazelnut bar for breakfast. "Can I go and call for Mirabelle and Cosmo, please? They're two of the travelling players I told you about, and they're coming to school with me today."

"Of course," said Mum.

Honey sprinted across to the Eyebrights' camp and found the troupe finishing breakfast on the grass beside the caravans.

"Is it time for school already?" Mirabelle asked, surprised.

"No. I came early to see if I could help out with anything," replied Honey.

"Great. We were just about to get the baskets of costumes down," Cosmo said. He grabbed a rope and scrambled up on to the caravan roof. Honey and Mirabelle climbed up after him.

Cosmo tied the rope through the handle of one of the baskets. "Grab hold," he said. Seizing the rope, Honey and Mirabelle lowered the basket to Caspar, who was waiting below.

Mrs Eyebright appeared as they were lowering the last basket. "Don't be late for school," she warned.

Honey had been enjoying herself so much that she'd forgotten about school. "We'd better run," she said. "Our teacher, Mr Hazelgrove, is pretty strict."

She, Mirabelle and Cosmo swung themselves down from the roof.

"After school, can you see if there's anywhere in the village that sells spider silk, Mirabelle?" said Mrs Eyebright. "I need to make your butterfly costume."

"I know somewhere, Mirabelle," said Honey. "Now let's go!"

They dashed across Primrose Meadow and arrived at school just as Mr Hazelgrove was calling everyone inside.

Florence, Evie and Natalie were waiting for them by the gate. "Thank goodness!" Evie exclaimed. "We thought you were going to be late."

They all ran into class.

"I've brought some new pupils for the week, sir," Honey said. She felt proud to be friends with real actors. "They're called Mirabelle and Cosmo Eyebright."

"Welcome," said Mr Hazelgrove.

Luke and Lily were at school, but Honey noticed a few empty places; the summer cold was obviously spreading. She wished Harvey would catch it so Mirabelle could sit next to her.

"Over there," said Mr Hazelgrove, directing Cosmo to a seat next to Monty Hornbeam. "And Mirabelle, you sit at the back."

The first lesson was basket weaving.

"Get into groups," said Mr Hazelgrove after he'd taken the register.

Honey jumped up eagerly. She'd be able to sit next to Mirabelle after all. Mirabelle, Cosmo and the friends crowded into the back row.

"This group's too big," said Mr Hazelgrove. "Evie, Natalie and Florence, move into the middle row."

The friends exchanged sorry glances as they did what they were told.

"You said you knew where I could buy spider silk, Honey," said Mirabelle, as they set to work weaving a foraging basket.

"The Buttercup Stitchery," Honey said. "I'll take you there after school. They've got—"

"Stop chattering, Honey," Mr Hazelgrove called sharply.

Honey waited until he'd turned away. "I'll tell you about it later," she whispered.

"Do you two like skipping?" Florence asked at playtime.

"Yes!" cried Mirabelle eagerly.

"No!" groaned Cosmo.

Monty Hornbeam came running up. He, Luke, Peter and Reggie were chasing each other around the playground. "Come and play tag with us, Cosmo," he said.

"Thanks!" Cosmo said. He waved to his sister and dashed off after Monty.

Florence shook out the long ivy stem rope. "Nat and I will turn the rope first."

"What do you do when you're not at school?" asked Mirabelle, as she skipped.

"We go sailing," said Florence. "We've got our own boat."

"And we have sleepovers in our secret den," added Evie in a low voice. "But don't tell anyone."

"We have loads of picnics, too," Natalie said. "And last winter we went sledging and made snow animals."

"Once a year we have a Summer Ball," Honey said. "It's only a couple of weeks away."

"How wonderful!" exclaimed Mirabelle. "You're so lucky to live here." She smiled at her new friends. "All that and skipping, too!"

Bluebell Woods

After school, as Florence took out her flute for band practice she sneezed loudly.

"Bless you," said Natalie. "I hope you're not coming down with this cold."

"One sneeze shouldn't stop me playing my flute," Florence replied.

"I can't stay for band practice," Honey whispered. "I'm taking Mirabelle to the Buttercup Stitchery."

"You'll get into trouble, Honey," warned Natalie. "You know we're working on that new song."

"It'll be OK," said Honey. "Do any of you want to come?"

"No, thanks," said Florence and Natalie together.

"I think the band would struggle without my woodblocks," Evie joked.

"Are you ready?" asked Mirabelle, coming over. "Cosmo's already gone home to learn his lines."

Mr Wintergreen, who ran the band, was getting out music stands, and Mr Hazelgrove was cleaning the blackboard. Neither was looking Honey's way. "Bye," she said hurriedly, and dashed across the classroom with Mirabelle hard on her heels.

"Wait, Honey, what shall we tell Mr Hazelgrove?" Evie hissed, but she'd already gone.

Mr Wintergreen finished putting out the music stands. "Half the band is missing," he said. "I suppose they've all caught this summer cold."

Florence grinned at Natalie and Evie. Perhaps Honey would get away with it. Then Mr Hazelgrove turned round. "Where's Honey?" he demanded.

"She … um … had to go straight home," said Evie.

"I shall speak to her in the morning," Mr Hazelgrove said crossly.

The friends sighed. Poor Honey was going to be in trouble after all.

Chapter Four

"What a brilliant shop!" cried Mirabelle, as she and Honey looked at the rows of coloured spider silks at the Buttercup Stitchery.

Mrs Buttercup came out of the back room. "I'm sorry, Honey, but I can't take on any more work before the Summer Ball."

"I haven't come about a ball dress," Honey said. "Mirabelle's buying some silk. She's one of the travelling players."

"Oh, hello, Mirabelle. What colour would you like?" asked Mrs Buttercup.

"Choose pink," said Honey.

"Maybe," said Mirabelle, twitching her whiskers thoughtfully. "I like this blue, but Cosmo's costume's blue."

"Pink's pale enough to be seen in the dark," Honey pointed out. "That's important for a midnight show."

"The lanterns will give plenty of light." Mirabelle lifted down a roll of yellow silk. "This one's pretty."

"But not as pretty as pink."

Mirabelle laughed. "OK, Honey. Pink it is!"

"Did you get the silk, Mirabelle?" asked Mrs Eyebright, when Honey and Mirabelle arrived at the players' camp.

"Yes." Mirabelle handed it over.

"What a lovely colour. It will go perfectly with these silver sequins." Mrs Eyebright sprinkled some on to the silk.

"Oh," gasped Honey. She'd never seen sequins before and she loved the way they glittered in the sunshine. "I wonder if Mrs Buttercup can get me some for my ball dress. I'm wearing the same one as last year so sequins would make it more special."

Mrs Eyebright measured Mirabelle, then went into the caravan to cut out the butterfly costume.

Cosmo came over with his play script.

"Have you learned your lines?" asked Mirabelle.

"Most of them." He flopped down on to the grass. "Do you want to know what happens in the play, Honey?"

"Yes, please," said Honey eagerly. She and Mirabelle sat beside him.

"I'm playing Danny Dormouse, the main character," Cosmo began. "And I'm lost in the woods. Other animals offer to show me the way out, but every time something goes wrong."

"Mirabelle, can I check a measurement?" called Mrs Eyebright.

"Back in a moment," Mirabelle said. She disappeared inside the caravan.

"Tell me about the other animals, Cosmo," said Honey.

"There's Robbie Rabbit, played by Caspar. Veronica will be Molly Mole and Tatiana's Lucy Ladybird."

"Tatiana?" Honey gasped. "She's only little."

"But she's talented," said Cosmo. "You'll get a surprise when she's on stage."

Honey felt a thrill of excitement. She loved surprises.

"In the end, Mirabelle's character, Bethany Butterfly, leads me home." He held out his script to Honey. "Will you help me practise?"

"Of course," Honey said. "Shall I read the other parts?"

"Yes, please. But we'll skip the songs."

Honey began to read, pausing when it was Cosmo's turn to speak. He knew most of his words and she only had to correct him twice.

43

Just as they reached the end of the play, Mirabelle came out of the caravan, beaming. "My butterfly costume's looking great," she said. "I'm glad I picked pink!"

"Me, too," Honey said, pleased.

"I don't feel well," croaked Harvey next morning.

Albie sneezed.

"Oh dear," Mum sighed. "You boys must have caught the summer cold. No school for you today."

Harvey started to say something, then clutched his neck. "My throat hurts when I talk."

"And mine," complained Albie.

"You'll both have to be quiet for once then!" Honey giggled.

"I'll make you a hot drink," said Mum, putting on the kettle. She fetched the honey pot from the larder and took off the lid. "Oh dear, this is almost empty, but I think there's just enough."

"See you later," Honey said, grabbing her school bag.

She ran to call for Mirabelle and Cosmo, and found Mr Eyebright pacing anxiously in front of their caravan.

"The show is doomed!" he exclaimed.

"Why?" squeaked Honey.

Mr Eyebright sat down on the caravan's step and buried his head in his paws. "Cosmo has a cold and, for the first time ever in the history of Eyebrights' Extravaganza, the show will not go on!"

45

Mrs Eyebright came hurrying between the caravans with a pawful of wild mint. "Whatever's wrong, Eduardo?" she asked.

"The show can't go ahead without its star," replied Mr Eyebright gloomily.

"Nonsense," Mrs Eyebright said. "It's not for three days. Cosmo will be better by then. I'll mix him some Mint Soother." Raising her voice, she called, "Will you bring me some honey, Mirabelle?"

Mirabelle came out of the caravan carrying a honey pot. "We've run out!"

"Please can you go and find some," said Mrs Eyebright. "Otherwise your father might be right about cancelling the show."

Mirabelle turned to Honey. "Do you know where there's a honey tree?" she asked.

"I remember Evie talking about one

in the woods. I sort of know where it is."
Honey sighed. "Harvey and Albie have got
colds and Mum gave them the last of our
honey this morning, otherwise she'd have
lent you some."

"I'm sure we'll find a beehive," said
Mirabelle. "Is there time to get there and
back before school?"

"Maybe," said Honey doubtfully. "We'd
better hurry."

They ran into Bluebell Woods. "This
way – I think," Honey said, setting off
along a narrow path.

It was cool and shady in the woods and
the birds were singing
sweetly as the two
friends scurried
along, looking
out for bees.

Bluebell Woods

After what seemed an age, they reached a place where the trees grew close together, blocking out the sunshine.

"Are you sure this is the way?" asked Mirabelle. "Bees like sunny, flowery places."

"It doesn't seem right," Honey admitted. She clambered on to a fallen tree and stretched up on tiptoe. "I can see sunlight up ahead," she squeaked. She jumped down and they hurried on.

Finally, they came to a clearing where foxgloves towered over them. "Bees!" cried Mirabelle, pointing.

"If we follow one it should lead us to its nest," said Honey.

They waited while the bees buzzed in and out of the foxglove flowers. At last, one flew across the clearing, heading for the trees on the far side.

"After it!" Honey yelled.

"I didn't realize bees could fly so fast," panted Mirabelle, as they reached the edge of the clearing.

The bee flew up into the air and joined a cluster of bees buzzing around a hole halfway up a tall oak tree. "We've found their nest!" Honey cried.

Keeping a careful eye on the bees, they climbed the tree. The nest was full of honeycomb, but as Mirabelle reached out for it the bees began to buzz angrily.

Mirabelle looked anxiously at Honey. "What can we do? We don't want to get stung!"

"I'll try to distract them," Honey said.

She scrambled down to the ground and ran into the clearing. The foxglove stems were too big for her to pick, but she gathered some low-growing clover flowers,

then raced back to the tree, waving them above her head. "Here, bees," she called. "Yummy nectar!"

The bees flew down to investigate as she scattered the flowers on the ground.

Up in the tree, Mirabelle quickly broke off a piece of honeycomb and placed it in her pot. Then she slid down and joined Honey on the ground.

"Thanks for distracting them, Honey," she said. "And for showing me the way."

"That's OK," said Honey. They'd been in the woods for ages and she was going to be terribly late for school, but at least now, hopefully, Cosmo would be better in time for the show.

Chapter Five

Honey and Mirabelle ran all the way back
to the Eyebrights' camp, but by the time
they arrived the sun was high overhead.

"It must be lunchtime," gasped Honey.
"I can't go to school now."

"I'm sorry, Honey," Mirabelle said.
"I shouldn't have asked you to help."

"It's not your fault," Honey said.

"Will you go home?" asked Mirabelle.

Honey shook her head. "I can't let Mum
and Dad know that I've missed school.
They'll be furious."

"Stay here then," said Mirabelle. "I'm working out my butterfly dance and I'm stuck on the last bit. Maybe you could help me with it. After we've had lunch, of course."

"I'd love to," said Honey. "But we'll have to keep behind the caravans. I don't want anyone spotting me."

Mrs Eyebright came out of the caravan. "Did you find any honey, girls?" she asked.

Mirabelle handed it over.

"Thank you. I've chopped the mint and wild garlic leaves so the cold remedy will be ready soon. Cosmo will be better in no time." As she went up the caravan steps, she glanced back. "You can take some

 home to your poorly brothers, Honey."

"Thanks," said Honey.

"Though actually I prefer it when they can't talk."

"It feels strange being at school without Honey and Florence," said Natalie, as she and Evie sat down to eat their lunch in the playground.

"Yes," Evie agreed. "The way Florence was sneezing at band practice, you could tell she was getting a cold. Though Honey seemed OK yesterday."

"It's bad luck for her to be ill at the same time as Harvey and Albie," said Natalie. "She won't get much peace and quiet at home." She unwrapped a chestnut pasty and bit into it.

"Let's go and visit both of them after school," Evie suggested.

"Good idea," Natalie said.

Bluebell Woods

"This is the bit of the dance I'm having trouble with," said Mirabelle. "How can I make Cosmo follow me?"

Freya was playing the butterfly music on her violin, and Honey had watched, enthralled, as Mirabelle performed the first part of her dance. She moved so gracefully that it was almost like watching a real butterfly.

"How about dancing all round Cosmo, then fluttering to the edge of the stage?" suggested Honey. The stage hadn't been built yet, but Mirabelle had marked out the space with stones.

"That's a brilliant idea!" Mirabelle exclaimed. "Will you stand here and pretend to be Cosmo? When the music slows, he asks me if I can show him the way out of the woods."

"Are you ready?" asked Freya.

Honey jumped up and Mirabelle danced around her, keeping in time to Freya's music, then skipped to the stone markers. "How did that look?" she asked.

"Perfect," said Honey.

"Right, I'll go through the whole thing again. And this time when I dance to the side, you follow me."

Mirabelle took up her sleeping-butterfly position, then Freya began to play. Mirabelle moved slowly at first, then leaped and spun as the music sped up. When the music  slowed, she looked expectantly at Honey.

"Can you show me the way out of the woods?" Honey asked, remembering Cosmo's line.

Mirabelle smiled, then danced round Honey before fluttering to one side, with Honey skipping after her.

"There," Mirabelle said. "Thanks for your help, Honey. I think I'm ready to show it to Mum and Dad now. I'll go and fetch them." She ran off.

"Time for a bit more violin practice," Freya said.

"I wonder if I can remember the steps," said Honey. She copied Mirabelle's sleeping-butterfly pose, then slowly woke up, stretching as she'd seen Mirabelle do, when Freya began to play. Soon she was twirling gracefully. As the music slowed, she paused, then danced round the spot

where Cosmo would be standing
and flitted to the side. As she
finished the dance, she heard
clapping and realized that
Mirabelle was watching.

"That was great, Honey."

Honey felt herself go hot with
embarrassment. "Thanks," she said,
pleased, though she knew her dancing
hadn't been nearly as good as Mirabelle's.
"Are your mum and dad on their way?"

"Yes. They just have to finish fixing
a lantern."

Honey peeped out from behind the
caravan and saw Monty Hornbeam
crossing Primrose Meadow. "School
must be over!" she gasped. "I'll have to
run home, otherwise Mum and Dad will
wonder where I've got to."

 "This is for your brothers," said Mirabelle, handing Honey a bottle. "It's my mum's Mint Soother."

"Thanks," Honey said. "Good luck with the dance practice, Mirabelle!"

As she came out from behind the caravans, she spotted Natalie and Evie walking towards her nest. *They must be coming to see me,* she thought. *And if they get home before I do, Mum and Dad will find out that I skipped school.*

Honey dashed towards her friends, yelling at them to stop.

They looked round in surprise. "What are you doing out here, Honey?" asked Natalie. "Are you feeling better?"

"I haven't been … ill," panted Honey.

"Were you skipping school?" asked Evie, shocked. "Honey, how could you!"

"It wasn't like that!" Honey explained what had happened. "And by the time we got back it was too late to go to school. I didn't want to get into trouble with Mr Hazelgrove."

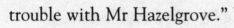

"You must have been worried," said Natalie.

"I was. And when I saw you…"

"You thought your mum and dad would find out," Evie said. "Lucky you caught us in time."

"Let's go and see Florence," said Natalie. "She wasn't at school either."

When they reached Florence's burrow they found her sitting outside in the sunshine, reading.

"How do you feel?" Evie asked.

Florence gave a big sneeze. "Not brilliant."

Honey held up the bottle of Mint Soother. "Have some of this. Mrs Eyebright made it for Cosmo, and she gave me some for Harvey and Albie."

While Evie knocked on Florence's front door to ask Mrs Candytuft for a spoon, Honey and Natalie sat down to tell her all about Honey missing school.

"Here," said Evie, coming back with the spoon.

Honey uncorked the bottle and measured out a spoonful for Florence.

Florence swallowed it. "Yuck!" she complained. "It tastes of garlic! Horrible!"

Honey grinned. "Good-o! There's plenty left for Harvey and Albie!"

Next morning, Harvey and Albie were yanking each other's tails when Honey went into the kitchen for breakfast.

"You boys are clearly better. That Mint Soother seems to have done the trick," said Mrs Pennyroyal. "Back to school today."

Harvey faked a sneeze. "We're still ill," he croaked.

"You don't fool me," tutted Mrs Pennyroyal. Sitting down, she wrote a note for Mr Hazelgrove, explaining why they'd been away. "There," she said, handing it to Honey. "You take it, Honey,

and make sure you give it straight to
Mr Hazelgrove."

Honey's paw trembled a little as she
took the note. She wasn't looking forward
to facing her teacher one bit.

Honey trudged across to the Eyebrights'
camp to call for Mirabelle. Cosmo was
better too, and the three of them walked
to school together.

"Did your mum and dad like the
butterfly dance, Mirabelle?" asked Honey.

"They loved it," Mirabelle replied.
"Especially the bit you suggested."

Cosmo and Mirabelle went on
chattering about the show, but Honey
hardly heard a word. She was trying to
work out what to say to Mr Hazelgrove.

They were nearly at school when they
met up with Natalie, Evie and Florence.

"That Mint Soother worked, Honey," Florence said. "I felt better almost as soon as you'd gone. Will you thank your mum for me, Mirabelle?"

"I hate to think what Mr Hazelgrove's going to say about yesterday," said Honey, as they went into the playground.

"You'll need an excuse for missing band practice, too," said Natalie,  putting her arm round Honey.

"I'd forgotten about that!" wailed Honey. "This is getting worse and worse."

Just then, Mrs Wintergreen called everyone into school. "Wish me luck," Honey said, as they went inside.

Chapter Six

Mr Hazelgrove was sitting at his desk. Taking a deep breath, Honey handed him the note.

He read it quickly, then looked up and smiled. "Are you feeling better now, Honey?"

Honey nodded, bewildered.

"Good. And I suppose you missed band practice because you weren't feeling well?"

"Um … yes."

"Right. Go and sit down."

Honey scampered to her place.

"He thinks the note's about me, too," she whispered to Evie.

"That's lucky," said Evie. "But don't skip school again."

"Don't worry, I won't!" Honey said.

"Is everything ready for the show now, Mirabelle?" Florence asked at lunchtime.

Mirabelle swallowed a mouthful of rosehip cookie and laughed. "There's still loads to do. Putting up the stage, painting the scenery... Oh, all sorts of things!"

"Can we help?" asked Natalie, brushing crumbs from her lap.

"That would be great," Mirabelle said, smiling. "Cosmo and I will be too busy for school tomorrow, but you can all come and help after lessons, if you like."

"Yes, please!" chorused the friends.

Bluebell Woods

Next day after school, when the friends reached Foxglove Hollow, Mirabelle came running over. "Thanks for coming. Will you help us paint the backdrops?"

"What are backdrops?" asked Evie.

"They're big pictures that hang behind the stage to show where the play is set. Come and see." Two large cloths hung from ropes strung between the caravans. One showed an outline of a woodland scene and the other a dormouse's nest.

"How lovely!" said Natalie. "Who drew them?"

"Leonie," Mirabelle replied. "She's an amazing artist."

Cosmo fetched pots of paint and brushes and handed them out. "Did we miss anything good at school today?" he asked.

"Not a thing!" exclaimed Evie.

They all laughed.

Florence, Honey and Cosmo set to work on the nest, while Evie, Natalie and Mirabelle painted the woodland scene.

"I've mixed the perfect shade of green for these oak leaves," said Natalie.

"Can I have some?" said Evie. Leaning down from her ladder, she dipped her brush in Natalie's paint pot.

Honey found herself humming while she painted.

"That's a pretty tune," said Florence.

"It's the music for Mirabelle's butterfly dance," said Honey. She loved the dance so much she'd been practising it at home in her bedroom.

"This is really good fun," said Evie, wiping a paint smudge from her paw. "Thanks for letting us help you, Mirabelle."

"Thanks for offering," Mirabelle said. "Otherwise me and Cosmo would probably have been up painting half the night."

When the backdrops were finished, they all stood back to admire them. "They look lovely," said Mirabelle.

"Can we go and see the stage please?" asked Honey.

Bluebell Woods

They ran down into Foxglove Hollow.
"Wow! It's bigger than I expected," said
Evie. The wooden stage was about three
times the size of one of the caravans.

"It has to be big enough for the whole
troupe," explained Cosmo. "Occasionally
we're all on stage at the same time."

They watched as Josiah climbed up
on to a wooden frame above the stage,
carrying a long rope. "What's that rope for,
Mirabelle?" asked Florence.

"You'll just have to wait until the
show," she said, before sneezing loudly.

"Are you OK?" Evie asked. "Your eyes
look watery."

Mirabelle went on sneezing.
"I ... think... Atishoo! ...
I've caught ... Atishoo! ...
the cold."

The friends exchanged anxious glances. "Let's take you back to your caravan," suggested Natalie. She slipped her arm round Mirabelle and they walked slowly back up the slope.

Mrs Eyebright was sitting on the caravan step, enjoying the last of the sunshine while she darned a sparkly jacket.

"I don't feel well," Mirabelle sniffed.

"Into bed with you and I'll fetch some Mint Soother," said Mrs Eyebright, putting down her sewing.

"Bye, Mirabelle," the friends said, as she climbed the caravan steps.

"I hope you're better in time for the show tomorrow," Honey added.

"What a day!" Honey groaned, as the friends walked home from school the next day. "I got told off five times for not concentrating."

"Well, you could hardly keep still!" giggled Evie. "It's not surprising Mr Hazelgrove noticed."

"I kept thinking about tonight's show," said Honey. "And wondering if Mirabelle's any better."

"I hope she is," said Natalie. "She looked really poorly yesterday."

They walked on in silence for a while, thinking about their friend.

"What time shall we go to Foxglove Hollow?" asked Florence, at last. "We want to get there in time to find a space near the stage."

"Let's head down there after tea," said Evie. "I'll knock for you all on the way."

"Good idea," the others agreed.

"Don't eat so quickly, Honey," said Mum. "You'll give yourself a tummy ache."

Honey swallowed her last mouthful of cherry pancake. "Sorry, but my friends will be here any moment."

There was a knock at the door. "That'll be them now," Honey cried, jumping up. "Can I go?"

"Yes," said Mum. "But calm down. You're like a whirlwind tonight!"

"Look for us near the stage," said Honey. "We'll save a space for you." Grabbing a cushion, she ran along the hall and threw open the front door. Florence, Evie and Natalie were outside. They'd brought cushions to sit on, too.

It was dusk and a few bats flitted overhead.

"They've hung curtains across the stage," cried Natalie, as they reached Foxglove Hollow. Lanterns hung above them and, as the daylight faded, they flickered magically.

Honey clutched Florence's arm. "This is going to be great, I just know it!"

Freya, Josiah and Leonie were already beside the stage, dressed in rainbow-coloured costumes. The strains of their music drifted up to the friends.

Bluebell Woods

"I wish I could play the flute as well as Josiah," said Florence.

"You will if you keep practising," Natalie said, squeezing her paw.

They skipped down the side of the hollow, following a path lit on either side by lanterns, and picked a place to sit close to the stage. Then they spread out, so there'd be plenty of room for their families, put down their cushions and made themselves comfortable.

Cosmo hurried past, wearing a sparkly blue suit.

"How's Mirabelle, Cosmo?" called Evie.

"Not great," he sighed.

"I'll go and try to cheer her up," said Honey. Before her friends could say anything, she jumped up and ran round behind the stage.

Mirabelle was
sitting on a box,
wrapped up in
a blanket. Her
eyes looked dull
and she was
hunched over.

"Hi," said Honey, trying to sound
cheerful. "Cosmo says you're still poorly."

Mirabelle sneezed. "My throat's sore,"
she croaked, "but at least I haven't got
any lines."

Mr and Mrs Eyebright came over.
"How do you feel now, sweetheart?" asked
Mrs Eyebright.

Mirabelle shrugged.

"Disaster!" exclaimed Mr Eyebright,
throwing up his hands. "We'll have to
cancel the show!"

"Someone else could play the butterfly," Mrs Eyebright said, frowning at him.

"No one else knows the dance," sighed Mirabelle. "I'll have to go on."

"I really don't think you should," said Mrs Eyebright. "You must rest." She scratched one ear thoughtfully. "We'll just have to change the ending. Tatiana can lead Cosmo out of the woods and we'll cut the butterfly scene altogether."

"The play will be too short if we do that," Mr Eyebright complained.

Suddenly, Mirabelle sat up a little straighter. "No, wait! Honey knows the butterfly dance."

They all looked at Honey.

"Will you go on instead of me, Honey?" asked Mirabelle. "It's the only way to save the show!"

Chapter Seven

Honey could hardly believe her ears. There was nothing she'd like better than to perform on a real stage, but it seemed so unfair on poor Mirabelle. "Won't you mind?" she asked.

"Of course not," Mirabelle said. "I'm always onstage." She looked hopefully at Honey. "Say you'll do it, Honey. Please!"

"Well, I suppose…" Honey trailed off. Could she do it? She'd practised the butterfly dance at home, but what if she forgot the steps once she had an audience?

"Wait," said Mr Eyebright. "We need to see how well Honey dances before we decide." He turned to Mrs Eyebright. "Will you fetch Freya?"

Freya came running with her violin, and Honey nervously took up the sleeping-butterfly pose. But as Freya began to play, the familiar music gave Honey confidence. Lifting her head, she stretched, then launched into the dance, swirling and twirling this way and that, then fluttering to the side as the dance ended.

"Marvellous!" exclaimed Mr Eyebright. "You're a worthy stand-in for Mirabelle."

"Come and change into the butterfly costume, Honey," Mrs Eyebright said.

It was hanging behind a screen, and Mrs Eyebright helped her to slip it on, then adjusted the glittery wings before leading her to the side of the stage. "Stay here in the wings till Cosmo comes across to call after Lucy Ladybird, dear," she explained. "Then creep on stage behind him, so the audience doesn't see you until he moves." She smiled encouragingly at Honey. "You can watch the rest of the show while you're waiting."

Mirabelle shuffled past, still wrapped in her blanket. "Good luck, Honey. I'm sure you'll be brilliant! I'm going to sit in the audience." She disappeared round the front of the stage.

Honey peeped through a narrow gap between the curtains, watching anxiously as the animals arrived.

Cosmo came to stand beside her. "Don't look so worried. You'll be fine," he said.

Honey clasped her paws together nervously. She hoped he was right. Part of her was looking forward to her big moment, but she wished she didn't feel so scared. What if she forgot the steps? Or worse, suppose she tripped over her own feet? The show would be ruined, and it would be all her fault.

"Honey's been a long time," said Florence.

Most of the audience had arrived now and they were waiting excitedly for the show to begin.

"Let's go and look for her," suggested Natalie.

The friends stood up, but just then their families appeared.

"This is a good spot," said Mrs Candytuft approvingly.

"Better sit down, girls," said Mrs
Hollyhock. "The show is about to start."

Mr Morningdew gave each of the
friends a bag of honeyed walnuts. "They
were selling these at the top of the slope.
We thought it would be nice to have
something to nibble while we watch
the show."

"Thanks," said Evie. "But we'll have
them when we get back, Dad. We're going
to look for Honey."

"Yes, I was wondering where she'd got
to. Where's she gone?" said Mr Pennyroyal.

"Backstage to—"

"I hope she's not being a nuisance,"
Mr Pennyroyal cut in sternly.

Freya hurried back with her violin and
the musicians played a fanfare.

"It's starting," whispered Florence.

They sat down on their cushions as Mr Eyebright emerged from behind the curtains. "Ladies and gentlemen, boys and girls, welcome to the Eyebrights' Extravaganza! Tonight we are proud to present our new show, *Lost in the Night*."

The audience applauded, but he held up a paw for silence. "Unfortunately, the performer playing the part of Bethany Butterfly is unwell."

"Poor Mirabelle!" whispered Natalie.

"So tonight the part will be played by a very special guest star." Mr Eyebright bowed low, then strode away out of sight.

"I wonder who the guest star is," Evie said quietly. "Poor Honey! She won't get to see much of the show from backstage."

Bluebell Woods

As the musicians began to play the curtains swished open, and they saw the woodland backdrop that Evie, Natalie and Mirabelle had painted.

Cosmo stumbled on to the stage. "I'm lost," he sighed. "I've been wandering this wood for hours. Will I ever see my family again?"

He started to sing:

"I came into the woods to find adventure.
I came into the woods to have some fun;
To climb some trees, pick woodland flowers,
To swing on creepers, play for hours,
And that is just exactly what I've done.
But now it's dark and I can't find the right path
To take me home. I want my mum and dad.
The trees all look the same at night
And screeching owls give me a fright.
I'm lost, alone and oh … so very sad."

Bluebell Woods

Just then, Caspar hopped on to the stage. "Hello," he said. "What's the matter?"

"I can't get out of this wood," sighed Cosmo.

The musicians struck up again and Caspar sang a jaunty song about knowing the woods inside out.

"So can you show me the way home?" Cosmo asked hopefully when the song ended.

"Of course! Follow me." Caspar raced off across the stage.

Cosmo started to follow, but Caspar jumped down into the audience. He dashed up the side of Foxglove Hollow and disappeared into the darkness.

"Wait!" Cosmo called from the stage. "I can't keep up."

"That's the trouble with rabbits," Evie joked, nudging Florence. "They run too fast!"

Next, the musicians played a slow, plodding tune and Veronica appeared. "You look sad, little dormouse," she said.

"I'm lost and I want to go home."

Veronica sang a song about knowing the secret tunnels beneath the woods. As she sang, she clapped her paws in time to the music and the audience joined in.

"Follow me," she said when the music stopped. She began to dig and, to the friends' amazement, a hole opened up in the stage floor. Veronica crawled into it.

"I can't go down there," wailed Cosmo, close to tears. "I'm afraid of the dark."

"Cosmo's a great actor, isn't he?" Natalie whispered.

"Yes," agreed Florence and Evie.

"Shhh," Hattie hissed, as the musicians began to play again.

Tatiana, dressed in her ladybird costume, toddled on to the stage.

"Can you help me get out of the woods?" cried Cosmo.

"This way," said Tatiana, pointing up at the sky. Suddenly, she flew into the air and swooped across the stage before disappearing into the wings.

"Oh!" cried Natalie, as the audience started clapping. "How did she do that?"

"I think she's attached to that rope Josiah was rigging up," Florence replied in a whisper.

"So that's why Mr Eyebright called her a Fantastic Flier," said Evie.

Cosmo waited until the applause had died down, then he called, "Wait! I can't fly!" Running to the side of the stage, he looked up in the direction Tatiana had taken. When he turned away sadly, the friends saw a butterfly asleep on the stage behind him.

"The guest star!" whispered Florence.

Cosmo began to sob loudly. Sleepily, the butterfly lifted its head.

"It's Honey!" the friends gasped.

Chapter Eight

Freya's violin sang out and Honey began to dance, stretching, then swirling to and fro across the stage, with her glittering pink wings spread wide. She tried not to think about the audience. Instead, she concentrated on the music, letting herself be swept along by it as she leaped high and swooped low.

"Can you show me the way out of the woods?" begged Cosmo, at last, as the music slowed.

Honey danced round him, opening

and closing her wings, then flitted to the
side of the stage. As
Cosmo came towards
her, she felt a thrill of
happiness. She'd done
it! She'd completed
the dance without
a single mistake!

As the curtains closed, she
slipped back into the wings of the stage.

"Well done, Honey," said Cosmo.
"That was terrific!"

"Thanks!" Honey beamed at him.

Mr Eyebright quickly changed the
backdrop, then the curtains opened to
reveal the dormouse's nest.

Cosmo scampered on stage. "Home
at last!" he exclaimed. He began his
final song:

Bluebell Woods

"I've been in the woods.
I went there to play.
But when darkness fell
I lost my way.
A kind butterfly
Took pity on me
She led me right home
In time for tea."

The curtains swished closed, and the audience clapped and cheered.

When they opened again, Cosmo grabbed Honey's paw and they ran out on stage with the other actors.

Honey smiled broadly as she curtseyed to the audience. She'd never dreamed that she would appear on a real stage with real actors and yet … here she was!

Mr Eyebright called Honey and Cosmo to the front of the stage. "Ladies and gentlemen, boys and girls, Cosmo Eyebright and our guest star, Honey Pennyroyal."

Honey curtseyed again as the audience gave them the biggest clap of all. Then the curtains closed.

With the applause still ringing in her ears, Honey quickly changed out of her butterfly costume. When she came out from behind the stage, she saw Florence, Natalie and Evie scampering towards her.

"Well done, Honey!" Evie cried.

"You danced brilliantly," Florence said.

"We're all so proud of you," said Natalie.

"I'm glad you liked it," said Honey. "And I'm sooo relieved it went OK."

Just then, Mirabelle appeared. "Congratulations," she said hoarsely. "I couldn't have done better myself."

Honey felt herself go hot with pride.

Mr Eyebright bustled over. "A thousand thanks, Honey. If you should ever wish to join us, I'll willingly find a part for you."

"I'm glad I could help," said Honey. She spotted her mum and dad, Hattie, Harvey and Albie heading her way, all smiling at her. "It's time to go," she said, feeling very tired suddenly. "But we'll come and see you before you leave tomorrow, Mirabelle."

She yawned widely as she went to meet her family. After all the excitement, she was well and truly ready for bed.

Next morning, when Honey arrived at the Eyebrights' camp, everything had been packed away and there was nothing but a rectangle of flattened grass where the stage had stood.

Mirabelle came running to meet her.

"How are you today?" Honey asked.

"Better!" she replied. She handed Honey a parcel wrapped in a dock leaf. "This is to say thanks for being a star."

Honey opened it eagerly. "Oh! Thank you!" she squeaked. Mirabelle had given her a box of silver sequins. "I'll sew these on to my ball dress."

"Bye, Honey," called Caspar and Leonie. "We're off now."

"So are we," said Josiah.

"Bye," Honey called back, waving madly as they set off towards the Babbling Brook, pulling their caravans. Freya and Veronica followed with the two carts.

Natalie, Evie and Florence came racing up. "Sorry," puffed Natalie. "I overslept, and Florence and Evie said they didn't mind waiting."

"Time to go," announced Mr Eyebright, lifting Tatiana on to the caravan seat.

He and Mrs Eyebright seized the shafts and began to pull. Mirabelle, Cosmo and the friends pushed from behind, and the caravan rolled forward.

"We're heading for a village in Campion Forest," said Mirabelle sadly.

"Aren't you excited about seeing somewhere new?" Honey asked. "I'd love a life like yours, living in a cosy caravan, putting on shows and—" She broke off, realizing that Mirabelle was staring at her in surprise. "What?" she said.

"I'd swap all that to live here in Bluebell Woods," Mirabelle said. "To stay in one place with friends like all of you would be amazing."

"But you wouldn't be onstage then," said Honey.

Mirabelle laughed. "Don't you ever put on shows in your village?"

Before Honey could answer, they reached the ferry and rolled the caravan aboard. Mirabelle hugged each of them in turn, then climbed up on the caravan roof to wave. "Goodbye," she called, as Mr Willowherb punted the raft away from the bank. "Don't forget me."

"We won't," the friends called together.

As the raft reached the far bank, Mirabelle gave one last wave.

"Mirabelle's right," said Natalie. "It's great having your friends around all the time."

"It is," agreed Honey, Evie and Florence, linking arms.

"She's right about putting on a show, too. We should do one for our parents," said Honey eagerly. "Let's start practising straightaway!"